Home At Last

Sofia's Immigrant Diary

· Book Two ·

by Kathryn Lasky

Scholastic Inc. New York

The North End, Boston
1903

April 3, 1903
The North End, Boston, Massachusetts

We live on the corner of Moon and Sun Streets. But there is no light here. Well, hardly any, just one ray of light in our apartment. It slithers in through the one window that faces Moon Street and it makes a patch of brightness in this dark place for half an hour each morning. But I am not complaining because now at last we have an address in America, Number 3 Moon Street, and I am sitting here eating Mama's tortellini soup. A month ago I had no address. I did not know where my mama and papa and sister and brothers were and I was eating garbage, although they called it food. Ha! Ha! I was locked up, but they called it "quarantined," in a jail, but they called it a "hospital" on Ellis Island in New York. They put me there because when our family arrived from Italy the doctors on that island thought I had an eye disease. They thought I would spread germs in America. It was stupid. I had no disease in my eye. Oh well, that is all over now.

There was one good thing, however, about that awful place. I made a best friend. A friend for life. Her name is Maureen O'Malley. They thought she had an eye disease, too. But now I am a little sad because Maureen is in Brooklyn, New York, and I am here in the North End of Boston. But Maureen and I promised to write each other. And somehow, some way, we shall see each other again. As Maureen said in her lovely Irish voice that makes every word sound like a song, "What is distance in miles, Sofia, when we have been able to know each other's thoughts before we could share one word?"

And that is the truth. I spoke no English and she spoke no Italian. But we had "shared hearts," as Maureen put it. You see, our hearts are linked forever. I feel close to her right now and that is why I write in this diary. I write in Italian, but sometimes a bit in English. I shall make a copy each day, and then collect the days and translate them as best I can into English and send them to Maureen in Brooklyn.

Tomorrow Papa starts his job at the Genovese grocery store. Friends of friends of a cousin back in Italy own the store. We are all to go with Papa because Mr. Genovese says we must have our picture taken together in front of his store to send back to the cousin and then they will know that we all got here safely. Mama snorted when she heard this. I do not know what she meant, really, by her snort, but when Mama snorts it usually is not a good sign.

April 4, 1903

I now know why Mama snorted. The Genoveses. They are the kind of family Mama snorts at. When Mama snorts it means somebody thinks they are better than they really are or know more than they really do. I heard Mama whisper, "*Molto arroganza*" under her breath as they were showing off the store. Mrs. Genovese was strutting about in her shiny patent leather shoes and fancy clothes. They are snortable. And so is their daughter, Mirella, who hardly spoke to me but kept smoothing the satin sash on her dress. She looked like she was dressed for mass, not a grocery store. Anyhow, we had our pictures taken in front of the store to send to our cousins, and the Genoveses were in the picture, too. But Mama said afterward that the real reason the Genoveses wanted this picture made was to show off what a nice store they have and what fancy clothes they all wear.

We looked terrible by comparison. Mr. Genovese in his starched collar and stiff cuffs poking out from his suit jacket stood next to Papa, who wore his patched pants and white shirt with no collar. Next was me in a baggy dress of Gabriella's that I have not yet grown into, standing beside Mirella with her satin sash. Mama in her long skirt and blouse with puffy sleeves all fresh and laundered but plain as a potato, and then Mrs. Genovese in her smart, dark red suit the color of wine with a fancy pin. She told us the pin was an award for her charitable work in a ladies' club to which she belongs.

It was a mistake when Mama asked what

the society did, for that was exactly what Mrs. Genovese wanted. "Oh, we help newly arrived immigrants. We help them find jobs and clothes." She looked straight at me. Then she added, "You know, so many of them are not just poor but brought up with no education or skills." Mama's face turned red as a tomato. I guess we are Mrs. Genovese's next charity project. She must be planning to collect another pin for the Monaris.

But this is a good job for Papa. Mr. Genovese says, "We are going to fix you up, Roberto. I have an extra collar and cuffs. Nice bow tie. You will look like a proper grocer."

Tomorrow we start school. Oh, and that is another thing. Mrs. Genovese thinks we should go to the Sacred Heart School but it costs some money. She says her club might be able to help. But Mama said no, absolutely not. In America education is free. That is the best thing about

America. We are to go to an American public school. There is one near our house. It is called the Paul Revere School. I have no idea why they call it that. Who was Paul Revere?

April 5, 1903

I love school. Gabriella hates it. We have been put in the same grade even though she is five years older. Gabriella turned fourteen last month and I am nine and we were both put in the third grade and that is only one grade above Luca, who turned eight last month and has been put in the second grade. I love my teacher. Her name is Miss Burnet. She is very tall and has piles of shiny brown hair that she pins on top of her head. Her eyes are very dark and twinkly and she has a dimple that flashes every time she laughs. She asked Gabriella and me to point on a map of Italy to our town. And our first lesson was to write in English our names and ages and where we come from. She said she would help us say and then spell the words. So I wrote, "My name is Sofia Monari and I come from Cento. I am nine years old." She kept asking us questions and we would say the answers and try to write them down, but Gabriella had a very hard time doing this. I now realize that Gabriella does not know nearly as much English as I do. That is the second good thing about when I was quarantined on Ellis Island. I learned a lot of English — mostly from Maureen. So I speak it a little bit with an Irish accent. But Gabriella knows none. And the Italian people in the North End speak a very funny kind of Italian. They speak in the dialect of either Sicilians or the Abruzzese. That is southern Italy and we come from northern Italy. So it is hard to understand them.

Oh, and I nearly forgot. Now I know who Paul Revere is — or was. He was one of the most famous Americans ever! During their Revolutionary War — another thing I never knew about — it was Paul Revere who rode out into the countryside to tell the people that the British were coming. But this is the best part of all. This I cannot believe. Paul Revere's house is practically next door to our house. Yes, if you come out of our apartment building, turn right, and walk straight about ten feet you come to North Square. Then walk another fifty feet or maybe one hundred and there is Paul Revere's house, except now it is a bank — Banco Italiana. Miss Burnet has told me that there is a wonderful poem called "The Midnight Ride of Paul Revere." She thinks it will be a very good way for me and Gabriella to learn English, so she is going to copy a part of the poem for us every few days.

April 6, 1903

I am so excited. Miss Burnet gave Gabriella and me the poem verse. I am copying it down right here and that will help me learn it even better. Then I am going to say it.

Listen my children and you shall hear
Of the midnight ride of Paul Revere,
On the eighteenth of April, in
    Seventy-Five;
Hardly a man is now alive
Who remembers that famous
    day and year.

Gabriella isn't even trying. This makes me so mad.

April 8, 1903

Mama took Marco with her to a place called the North Bennet Street School. They have a day nursery, and while the children are watched the mothers can learn things. I'm not sure what. Mama knows so much already. But I guess they give a class in speaking English and Mama wants to learn because she says no one understands her Italian. The classes are free. She said many of the women, however, are learning how to sew and clean there. I said, but Mama, what woman doesn't know how to sew and clean? That just seems stupid to me to have to go to school to learn that. And she said they learn it in a special way so they can be maids in the rich peoples' houses in Boston. She said there are many Irish girls who take these classes. The rich ladies of Boston like Irish maids, she said. I hope Mama doesn't do this. I just want her to learn English. That's all. Then stay home and cook and clean for us.

April 10, 1903

Easter is this Sunday. Mr. Genovese gave Papa a leg of lamb to cook. Well, didn't exactly give it to him. Papa has to pay half the price. Papa said that he thinks that Mr. Genovese would have given it to him for free but that Mrs. Genovese made him charge Papa.

April 11, 1903

All day Mama is cooking for our first Easter dinner in America. Gabriella and I help her cut the tagliatelle. She is worried that the wheat flour is not fine enough here in America. "It must be very light," she keeps saying. "Tagliatelle must float on your tongue."

And then she makes the special dough for the Columba buns — the dove buns, for they look a little bit like fat birds. We "feather" their wings with thin sliced almonds and use whole almonds for their eyes. Mama gives Marco some dough to play with. Luca is playing with a boy, Fredo, across the hall who is in his class. He is learning a lot of English from him. I wish Gabriella would make a friend and learn English. She doesn't want to learn from me because I am her younger sister. And in our class there are only younger girls. So I don't know how she will make a friend her own age. I don't really care for myself. I just want to be Miss Burnet's friend.

April 12, 1903

Today is Sunday. The smell of lamb roasting woke me up. That is all one smells in the North End. And since it is warm, people cook with their windows open.

Went to mass at the Church of the Sacred Heart, which is almost across the street from us. The Genoveses were there. You should have seen Mrs. Genovese's hat. That is about all I saw because she sat in front of me and the feathers stuck up about two feet high and I couldn't see the priest at all. Mirella had on a dark blue velvet dress with silk rosebuds on the collar. I thought it looked kind of babyish.

Papa wore the collar and cuffs that Mr. Genovese gave him for work to church, and he looked very handsome because he wore his old frock coat over it instead of his grocer's apron. Even though the coat is worn he still looked good. Mr. Genovese seems very nice but I really do not like Mrs. Genovese. She is one of those people who even when she tries to sound nice sounds insulting. For example, she came up to Mama and said in front of Papa, like a teacher would say about a child, "Mr. Genovese tells me that Roberto is doing a very fine job. You must be so proud of him." I cannot exactly describe why I find this insulting, but it is, believe me.

Our Easter dinner was good. Mama cooked the lamb perfectly and the dove buns were nice and buttery and the tagliatelle floated on our tongues. Papa said the only thing we needed were some good Cento tomatoes. Mama made a cassat cake for dessert and the sweet cream was so good, but she left out the candied fruits. She said they are too expensive. The candied fruit pieces make the cake prettier. They sparkle like jewels when you slice it. Oh well.

Later

I have thought about Mrs. Genovese. I know what she should have said instead. First of all, she should have said "Corrado," for that is Mr. Genovese's first name. She feels it is fine to call Mama "Angelina" and Papa "Roberto," but we are expected to call them Mr. and Mrs. But to go on. She should have said, "Angelina, Corrado says that Roberto is so wonderful, he wouldn't know what to do without him now." Period! None of this "you must be so proud!" You say that about children, not adults. I know Mama is proud of Papa. She does not need the likes of Thomasina Genovese to tell her. I am only going to call Mrs. Genovese Thomasina from now on — at least in this diary. Maybe I shall even call her Tomi.

April 13, 1903

Another verse from the Paul Revere poem:

He said to his friend, "If the British
*   march*
By land or sea from the town to-night,
Hang a lantern aloft in the belfry arch
Of the North Church tower as a signal
*   light, —*
One, if by land, and two, if by sea:
And I on the opposite shore will be,
Ready to ride and spread the alarm
Through every Middlesex village and
*   farm,*
For the country-folk to be up and to
*   arm."*

What in the world is a belfry?

Later

A belfry is a bell tower, a *campanile!* And guess who found the answer? Mama. Her teacher at the North Bennet Street School loaned her an English-Italian dictionary.

Later

Oh my goodness, the worst thing happened. Little Marco tore a page in the dictionary. Mama is so angry. Papa says he will get some special glue from the grocery store and mend it. I don't know how he will ever do that. There is such a racket in this small apartment my head aches. Marco is howling because Mama swatted him. Mama is crying. Papa is shouting that he can fix it. Gabriella is screaming at Luca because she said he peed in the tub water and she refuses now to bathe in it. He probably did. Mama now yells that she is not heating up new kettles of water. We have used our wood supply for the week. Papa shouts for her to use another piece of wood — who wants to bathe in Luca's dirty water? And why does Luca have to be such a lazy boy and not hold it and go to the toilet down the hall? Oh my goodness, we haven't had a family fight like this since Cento, when Luca and his friend Pietro were chasing the pig for Saint Anthony's Day and it fell into a lake and drowned! And all I want to do is have peace and quiet and learn the verse to the poem that Miss Burnet wrote out for me. But still, I'd rather be here with my screaming, crazy family than in that hospital on Ellis Island. I do miss Maureen, though. Tomorrow I am copying these pages and sending them to her. I bet Miss Burnet's family doesn't have fights like this. I bet they never raise their voices. Of course, I don't know a thing about Miss Burnet's family. I don't even know if she has a family or where she lives.

April 14, 1903

Oh my goodness, I know so much about Miss Burnet! Miss Burnet went to a college called Radcliffe that she says is across the river from Boston in a town called Cambridge. And she lives there with her mother and father and younger brother who goes to Harvard, which is a very famous college and the oldest college in America. You have to be very smart to get into it, I think. And her father teaches at Harvard. He is a professor of astronomy. He studies the stars! Imagine getting paid to study the stars. Why, I think this is the most wonderful thing I have ever heard.

Now the reason I found out all this is because Miss Burnet says she is very worried about Gabriella. She says Gabriella does not have a good attitude about learning and that she wishes she were an eager student like me. She would like to promote me to the fourth grade. But she does not know what to do about Gabriella. So she has asked me to have Mama come in and talk to her, but I shall have to come with Mama to translate.

P.S. I mailed a copy of my pages to Maureen. I copied them on very thin paper so I could mail them for a penny.

April 15, 1903

This is a terrible problem. Mama does not think that I should be promoted and put in a grade higher than Gabriella. But I want to be promoted. Why should I have to wait for old Gabriella who doesn't care a bean about learning?

April 16, 1903

Oh, my problem might be solved. Gabriella has made a friend. A girl she met when she was taking Marco for a walk. This girl works at the Samoset chocolate factory on Hanover Street. She dips chocolates all day long and makes bonbons and caramels, and she gets paid thirty cents an hour! I think this might be a good idea for Gabriella.

Later

Mama does not. Mama and Papa say that education is free here in America and Gabriella has the rest of her life to work and that we are lucky because Papa has a good job and we children do not need to work. I'll never get promoted.

April 17, 1903

Gabriella does not give up. She said that if a girl or boy is fourteen years old and works they still must go to school. It is called continuation school and they go one half day a week. So she is going to tell Mama and Papa this to see if now maybe they will let her work. I am keeping my fingers crossed.

Later

No. Mama and Papa says a half day once a week is not enough to learn properly. And Papa says that you have to weigh at least ninety pounds to work if you're a child and

Gabriella is very skinny. I bet she doesn't weigh eighty-five pounds.

April 18, 1903

Gabriella does not quit. She says the chocolate girl doesn't weigh ninety pounds but that her sister got her these lead disks from the shoe factory where she works. She put the disks in her shoes to make her weigh more.

Mama and Papa really had a fit! They were yelling at her that they did not raise a child to tell lies. Then Gabriella says that is not telling a lie. There is this whole argument about whether putting lead in your shoes is the same as telling a lie. It is the stupidest argument I have ever heard in my life. Luca says he thinks that it is dishonest. Then Gabriella turns on Luca and says, "What do you know?" And Luca bites Gabriella! And Papa smacks Luca.

Holy Mother, all I want to do is learn the next verses of the Paul Revere poem. This is the loudest family.

April 21, 1903

Job idea number thirty-six for Gabriella: ladies' maid. She seems to come up with a new idea for work every hour. She and I went to meet Mama at the North Bennet Street School and while we were waiting for her Gabriella starts talking to this girl, Antonia, and Antonia's friend who is Irish comes up. There are not many Irish people living in the North End, but this girl Molly is taking sewing classes here because she wants to become a maid like her big sister. So now Gabriella wants to become a maid and wants to take sewing classes.

April 24, 1903

Miss Burnet wants to see Mama again. I am so worried. This is so embarrassing having a sister like Gabriella. She is making a mess of my life. I told Mama that and Mama became very angry with me. She said, "She is making a mess of her own life!"

Later

I feel terrible. I told Gabriella what Mama said. I expected her to get mad, but she did something worse. She started to cry. "Do you know what it's like to be with kids half your age and half your size? I might be skinny but I am three feet taller than those kids. You're just a year older and you're short for your age anyhow. I can't stand it. They laugh at me. They tease me because my little sister and my little brother speak better English than I do. How would you feel?"

Well, I feel terrible. I guess I don't even want to be promoted anymore. I'll learn what the fourth graders are learning on my own, somehow. I'm saying good-bye to the promotion. *Arrivederci*, fourth grade.

April 26, 1903

I cannot believe this idea that Miss Burnet came up with. It might be wonderful or it could be a complete disaster. Miss Burnet thinks that Mama should allow Gabriella to take sewing lessons because they are taught in English and she will be more willing to learn if it is a subject that she has chosen. But this is the amazing part. She wants to promote Gabriella to the seventh grade! And me to the fourth grade. She says that Mama should tell

Gabriella that as long as she tries to learn in school and do her schoolwork she will be permitted to take the sewing lessons. Mama and I both wonder how Gabriella will be able to do seventh grade work. Miss Burnet says she will want to keep up with girls who are more her age and that the teacher, Miss Drew, is very good and will give her extra help.

So now Gabriella is ahead of me. I guess that is right. But I at least got to be promoted. *Ciao*, fourth grade! I sure hope Gabriella does what she is supposed to do.

April 28, 1903

I don't like the fourth grade teacher nearly as much as Miss Burnet. Her name is Miss Coggins. She wears a wig and it keeps slipping. She is always pushing it around on her head. And she is awfully strict. She makes us sit with both our feet flat on the floor. We are not allowed to cross our ankles. She says it is not proper and she doesn't want to see the bottom of our shoes. But there is a nice girl in the class. Her name is Chiarina. She speaks very good English and her mother used to go to the North Bennet Street School. She says that she belongs to one of the clubs for Italian girls at the school. So I might go with her one day. Then she asks if my brother is Luca. And I say yes and how does she know that. And she says, "Everyone knows Luca." And I say how. And she says, "He gets around." I do not know whether this is good or bad. I will say one thing. I noticed that Luca's English has improved a lot since we've been here.

May 4, 1903

I think Miss Burnet's plan might be working! Gabriella is really studying hard. She even asks me for help with her English. She is learning a lot of sewing words like "needle" and "treadle" and "spool" and "hem" and "baste." I told her that she should make up a list of new English words like I did when I was on Ellis Island. I showed her my list. She looked at all the words as if she had never seen anything like it. I said, "Gabriella, they are just words. It is not poetry like the Paul Revere poem." And all of a sudden she says that she wants to learn that poem now, too. So I get out of my copies that Miss Burnet had made and she gets out her old ones and I read them aloud to her. I sort of explain the story half in English and half in Italian, and then I show her the new verse that Miss Burnet gave me this week. You see, even though I am no longer in Miss Burnet's class, she still gives me the verses.

May 5, 1903

It has been two weeks since I sent the copies of my diary pages to Maureen and I haven't received anything from her. I hope she is all right. I hope she hasn't forgotten me. When Maureen and I were in the hospital on Ellis Island we both secretly worried that our families would forget about us. That we would just fade away in their minds. That, I think, was my worst nightmare — being forgotten.

I like Chiarina a lot, but it's not the same as it was with Maureen. It could never be the same with anybody as it was with Maureen. I mean, we were both in prison together, after all!

But still Chiarina is nice, and this Saturday she is going to take me with her to the meeting of her club. They call themselves the Lilies of the Arno. I think that is such a pretty name. The Arno is a river in Italy. I have never seen it, but Papa has. It flows through the city of Florence.

May 6, 1903

Well, now I know what Chiarina meant when she said that Luca gets around. Guess who has a job? Luca! All the time Gabriella was talking about getting a job Luca is the one who got one. He started shining shoes down on the waterfront, on Atlantic Avenue. We asked where he got the money for shoe polish and brushes and all the things he needs? He says each week he pays part of what he makes to a bigger boy who has "rented" him the equipment. Now this week he shows us that he has made two dollars! Two whole dollars!

Mama is worried. She doesn't want Luca to do it. Papa says as long as he goes to school and studies hard, what is the harm? I think Papa won this argument. I think Papa is proud of Luca. And I think the rest of us can hardly believe it. I mean, little Luca — a businessman?

May 7, 1903

Papa likes his job but he does not like Mrs. Genovese. He says she comes in all the time and is always rearranging stock and criticizing Mr. Genovese. Papa says Mr. Genovese is henpecked. He says no real Italian man would stand for this. Mama snorts.

May 8, 1903

I went to the Lilies of the Arno meeting. It was so much fun. I am going to join. We are planning a puppet show, and then we started talking about what we shall do for the feast of Saint Anthony in August. They make a very big affair in the summertime out of the saints' days here in the North End. They have parades and lots of food and dancing. The girls in the club are very nice.

Oh, I nearly forgot! Mama took back the dictionary. Papa did fix it beautifully but she was so nervous that she brought her English teacher some of her tortellini. The teacher, Miss Bradshaw, was very pleased and she had Mama write out in English the instructions for cooking the tortellini. So Mama wrote in English, "Bring water to boil. Add tablespoon of salt. Put in tortellini. Cook until *al dente*."

Mama said she didn't know how to translate *al dente*. She tried to explain by pointing to her teeth. There didn't seem to be an exact word in the Italian-English dictionary. Finally, Miss Bradshaw said, "Tender?" Mama thinks that "tender" is the best word so far, but she is not sure if Miss Bradshaw really understands. It is not tender like meat. It is tender in a way that only pasta can be tender, and Mama does not think Americans like Miss Bradshaw understand this.

May 10, 1903

We are invited this afternoon to Mrs. Genovese's for tea. I don't want to go. But Mama said we have to. Luca didn't have to because of his "business." Now in addition to shining shoes he got, through his friend Arturo, a job delivering newspapers to the ships down on the wharves. He has only been doing this for two days, but on Saturday the sailors on one ship invited him to stay for dinner. He is so lucky! This is a great city to be a boy in. I mean, I like the Lilies of the Arno and planning puppet shows, but Luca just runs all over the place, makes money, and has adventures like eating on ships with names like the *North Star*. I think that is so thrilling. I asked him to take me but he says girls aren't allowed.

Later

Tea at the Genoveses was a catastrophe! We wound up rushing with Marco to a doctor's office. You'll never guess what that baby boy did. Wait. I jump ahead. Just imagine we are there in the Genoveses' fancy two-floor apartment on Fleet Street. Very grand. Ornaments all over for Marco to break — Venetian glass and something Mama called flocked wallpaper and lots of velvet curtains with gold-colored fringe. Mrs. Genovese — pardon me, Tomi — is so stuck-up and so is her daughter, Mirella. I knew Mama wasn't liking it any better than I was. She nearly snorted out loud a couple of times, especially when Tomi was talking about their "summer place — up north." From the way she kept repeating "up north," I thought she meant someplace like the North Pole, which Miss Burnet showed us on the map. And the real name for the North Pole is the Arctic Circle. So finally I said, just trying to make conversation, "It must be very cold for you, even in the summer. I mean, they say there are still icebergs in the Arctic in the summertime." Tomi just stared at me. "What are you talking about?" she finally said. "We go to Revere Beach, not that frozen place!"

Mama giggled and Tomi shot her a fierce look. Then Tomi told Mirella to take me and Gabriella and Marco to see her doll collection. Marco was being very whiny and cranky. Mirella would not let us touch any of the dolls. "They are collector dolls," she announced. "They are very fragile. They have bisque heads and moveable eyes."

Well, just as I am thinking how much fun I was having — oh, I thought I would die of amusement, admiring a rich girl's doll collection — I hear Mirella scream, "He's eating my doll. He is eating my doll! The little ———." And she called Marco a very bad name. But of course Marco just smiled, his cute chubby face dimpling up, and then he swallowed. And you could just about hear the gulp as the doll's eyeball went down. Yes, Marco swallowed that stupid doll's moveable eye. I guess it looked like a piece of candy to him and he plucked it out of the doll's face.

Well, everyone started screaming. Tomi and Mama ran in. Tomi picked Marco up and held him upside down just as if he was a saltshaker and started shaking him. Mama flew at Tomi and grabbed Marco. Marco was wailing. Then Tomi said, "Quick, take him to Dr. Balboni. He will know what to do."

So she sent the maid with us to show us where the doctor's office was on Prince Street. Dr. Balboni came out of his office when he heard all the noise. And now this is the best part of the whole story. Mama is wailing in Italian, of course, and I am trying to translate as fast as I can, and Dr. Balboni lifts his hand for us to be quiet and says in Italian, beautiful Italian, "Wait a minute. I can tell by your accent you are from Cento." And we can tell from his accent that he also is from Cento. Oh my goodness, I thought Mama would kiss him right there. Then we all go into his office and he examines Marco. Marco calms down immediately because Dr. Balboni took a small medallion on a chain that he wore on his neck and gave it to Marco to play with. He says to Marco, "Now don't swallow this, young fellow." But next he does the funniest thing ever. He takes off his spectacles and puts them on Marco's tummy. "So the eye can see. These doll's eyes are very short-sighted." Well, we all start laughing so hard.

He tells Mama that Marco shall be fine. That it is not obstructing anything. The worst that could have happened — choking — didn't happen. And that we should be patient and "everything will come out fine." Then stupid me says, "How?" And Mama and the doctor laugh and I turn as red as a tomato. For now I know what he means. Nature will take care of it, and the eyeball will come out on its own. Charming! When we leave, the doctor refuses any payment for the visit. He gives Mama a slip of paper written in Italian that tells her about the milk and baby hygiene clinic that is here in the North End. The clinic teaches women how to pasteurize their milk so that babies won't get that awful disease from some germ that can be in milk. Mama says that she will go. When we leave and Dr. Balboni puts his medallion back on I notice that it is a Saint Christopher's medal.

There is one person who is not so patient. Tomi! That woman is terrible. She wants her husband to deduct money from Papa's wages every week until the cost of a new eye for the doll is paid.

May 12, 1903

Mama has been cooking for two days. She is making some tortellini for Dr. Balboni and she is — I cannot believe this — giving him our last jar of sun-dried tomatoes from Cento that she dried herself and brought all the way here. She is also making him some bread, but she is going to send me to the bakery over on Fleet Street with the dough to be baked. She does not think our oven bakes good enough for the doctor, and the Fleet Street bakery will do this for two cents. So I am to take it now, and then I shall come back for it in two hours. Fleet Street is the same street that the Genoveses live on. I am so scared I shall see Tomi or that awful Mirella.

May 13, 1903

Yesterday turned out to be a really good day. After I picked up the bread I took it, the tortellini, and the sun-dried tomatoes to Dr. Balboni's office. He had just seen his last patient of the day and he seemed truly pleased with the basket of food Mama had sent. He invited me in and said, "Sit down, tell me about yourself, Sofia." He asked what I was studying in school and what I liked the most. He talked to me as if I were not just some kid, but the way a grown-up talks to another grown-up. Then he said something that really startled me. He said, "Now Sofia, what might you hope to be or do some day?" Well, no one has ever asked me that. I did not even know this was a question that could be asked. I was not even sure what he meant.

My silence seemed to fill the room. He

leaned forward and looked me straight in the eyes. "Sofia," he said. "This is America. There are many things you can be. I have a friend, a lady friend, who is a nurse at the Massachusetts General Hospital. She is a wonderful operating room nurse. She has a friend who is a secretary to the president of the largest bank in Boston."

It was so strange. I thought of all the jobs Gabriella wanted. The one in the chocolate factory, the maid in a fancy Boston house. But those are just jobs. I do not think this is what Dr. Balboni is asking — not what job I want, but what I want to be. There is a big difference. So I told him that I would have to think about it. And he said that is the best answer because in order to think about it and make a good decision I shall have to keep studying very hard. He complimented me on my English.

May 14, 1903

Mama's teacher, Miss Bradshaw, at the North Bennet Street School loved the tortellini so much that she has offered to pay Mama for another batch and so has her friend Miss Gillespie, who is the secretary at the school. Mama doesn't know how much to charge. Papa says she should charge twenty cents a pound. That is what the pasta shop on Hanover Street charges and Mama's is much better. Mama says that is too much. She will only charge fifteen cents. By the way, Mr. Genovese sent the eye back. He says his wife won't have it in the house. I don't know what we are to do with it. The good news is that Mr. Genovese is *not* going to take money out of Papa's wages. He is just going to pretend to his wife that he is. Papa asked Mama if she could make an extra half pound of tortellini to take to Mr. Genovese, as he has really been so nice.

I think Mama is going to be making tortellini every hour of every day.

May 16, 1903

She *is* making tortellini every hour of every day! Imagine our surprise when just after supper last night there is a knock on our door, and when we open the door who is standing there but Dr. Balboni. He takes off his hat and bows deeply to Mama. "Signora," he says, "I have never in my life tasted such marvelous tortellini or such wonderful sun-dried tomatoes. I have a lady friend and she never really liked Italian food until I cooked her your tortellini and made a sauce with the sun-dried tomatoes. She nearly swooned with delight."

Oh my goodness, Mama was so excited she

nearly cried. To have an elegant man, a doctor like Gerardo Balboni, no less, complimenting her cooking, well, Mama nearly swooned. And then Marco came toddling in and Dr. Balboni turns to him and says, "Marco, how can you eat the eyeballs of silly dolls when your Mama makes tortellini like this? Keep away from the eyeballs, Marco." We all laugh and Papa invites Dr. Balboni for a little cup of wine. *Vin Santo.* I never see Papa bring out this wine except at Christmas and on very special occasions.

It was very exciting having such a gentleman in our apartment. I wished Tomi could see us now. That was what I was thinking.

May 17, 1903

It has been over a month since I sent my letter to Maureen and still no answer. I am very sad. I think I am fading away in her mind.

May 20, 1903

I went to another Lilies of the Arno meeting with Chiarina. We had a lot of fun. Mrs. Del Orio, whose daughter is in the group and leads us in a lot of the projects, brought in a set of American and Italian flags and gave us silver and gold thread. We are going to embroider them with the thread. Then on the Sunday before Independence Day on the Fourth of July, the big American holiday, we will bring the flags to the church and the priest will bless them in a service that is called the Baptism of the Flags. And then on the Fourth of July we get to ride on a float and wave the flags. I am so excited. I think I shall feel like a real American.

May 21, 1903

Mr. Genovese liked Mama's tortellini so much that he has asked her if she would make three or four pounds for him to sell in the store. He will charge twenty cents a pound and Mama can keep seventeen cents! And there are more orders from other ladies at the Bennet Street School.

May 22, 1903

Mama sent me over to Dr. Balboni with some more tortellini. She was making so much she said why not send over a pound for him and his lady friend? I wonder what Dr. Balboni's lady friend is like?

May 25, 1903

Gabriella is doing very well in her new grade. Her English has improved. She nearly caught up with me on learning the Paul Revere poem. She loves her sewing classes and now wants to take cooking. Then she says she shall make a perfect maid for a rich Boston family. I am very happy that Gabriella is doing so well. But I am sad that I have not heard from Maureen. I have this terrible fear that something might be wrong. Why, when I stop worrying about Gabriella, do I have to start worrying about Maureen? Why can't everybody be just fine all at the same time?

May 30, 1903

We only have about three more weeks of school left. I think I shall be sad when it ends.

I shall miss seeing Miss Burnet, not Miss Coggins. She is very grouchy. Still no letter from Maureen.

May 31, 1903

Mama is so busy with her tortellini. Now it seems to me that everyone is very busy in our family except me. Luca has his two jobs and is always talking about eating on ships. He says the tugboats have the best food. Gabriella is always with her friend Molly. She even went to church with Molly last Sunday. All the Irish who live in the North End go to Saint Stephen's Church up on Hanover Street. Gabriella said that there was this beautiful girl in church, one of the most beautiful girls she has ever seen and just her age. She said that Molly told her the girl's name was Rose Fitzgerald and that she was the daughter of

Honey Fitz — isn't that a funny name? Honey Fitz. His real name is John Fitzgerald and *he used to be a congressman*. All this talk about Irish people makes me miss Maureen even more.

June 3, 1903

Today after our meeting of the Lilies of the Arno one of the girls from the Jewish club, the Wiltsie Club, started talking to us. She was so nice. Her name is Mirka. We admired her scarf and she said that it came from her father's shop on Salem Street. She invited us to come and see the store. So we went. I have never been to Salem Street. It was as if I had walked into another world. I heard some Italian but then there was another language I had never heard. Mirka said it is Yiddish. But she said I might also hear some Russian. There were meat shops with signs in letters that looked nothing like the alphabet. Mirka said those letters were Hebrew and the shops were kosher butcher shops. Chiarina said her mother always buys her meat in Salem Street because these butchers are known to have the freshest meat. The street is very narrow and jammed with people — more people than on Hanover Street on a Saturday morning. And that is a lot of people. There is one very large building, a department store called Jordan Marsh, and at first I thought this was Mirka's father's store but she laughed and said no. We went another half block and came to the Cohen Dry Goods Store. This was Mirka's father's shop. They had very nice things.

Then Mirka said we should come up to their apartment. Her mother was very sweet. She offered us tea and brought out a plate of cookies that she called *rugulah*. They had dabs of apricot jam in the center and were really good. Mrs. Cohen asked us if we knew anyone interested in a small but very easy job. So I asked what. She explained that on the Friday Sabbath Jews cannot light fires — not cook fires, not lamps to see by, or anything, and that she needed someone to come at sundown and light the fires. So Chiarina and I immediately said we would do it. She said she would pay us each ten cents! But first we must check with our parents. Ten cents! I can't believe it. That is almost as much as Mama gets for her tortellini. I am so excited. I hope Mama and Papa let me do it.

Later

Mama and Papa say I can do it. And you know what? I can already see that Luca is interested. He started asking me all about Salem Street and the Jewish people who live there. That kid is going to be a millionaire by the time he's fifteen.

June 5, 1903

My first earned dime in America! Chiarina and I completed the job! It was fun. We had to light the burners for a soup to simmer on and then there were at least fifteen oil lamps to light. When we left, fog rolled in from the harbor and all the edges of the buildings on Salem Street had grown soft and fuzzy. But when we stood in the street and looked up we could see the lamps we had lit glowing in the Cohens' window above their store. It gave us a nice feeling to know we had helped them. They would have hot soup because of us and hot tea and a kettleful of hot water to wash their face and hands as well. Chiarina and I decided not to go straight home but to explore this side of the North End, for neither of us knows it very well. So we went first to the Copps Hill burying ground. You have to walk straight up Hull Street, which is very steep, to get there, and at the top there is a nice view of the Charles River and even Charlestown, but it was too foggy to see much.

Miss Coggins told us that the British used Copps Hill, from where they fired their cannons during the Revolutionary War, in the Battle of Bunker Hill. We couldn't see Bunker Hill tonight because of the fog, but I guess it is not that far away. Then we walked back through the yard of the Old North Church. The fog was now so thick you couldn't even see the steeple. It was lucky they had a clear night when the man lit lanterns to signal that the British were coming by sea. When we came to the statue of Paul Revere in the churchyard it looked as if his horse were prancing through the clouds. The fog swirled in so thick for a minute that it suddenly seemed as if Paul had no horse under him at all. It was as if he was just magically suspended in air. It was the strangest thing.

Miss Burnet gave me the next verse of the Paul Revere poem, and — this is the most exciting of all — after school finishes she is going to take me to Cambridge and show me the house of the poet Mr. Henry Wadsworth Longfellow who wrote this poem. I can't wait.

June 7, 1903

Finally a letter from Maureen. But it is rather a sad letter. My hands were trembling when Mama handed it to me. I must have stared at the envelope for a good three minutes. I just looked at my name — the letters printed by my dearest friend. I closed my eyes and thought about how Maureen's fingers had held this envelope, touched the page, and then I opened it. The news is very, very sad. Her father has not found work yet. Her mother is ill. And the worst is that she says they talk about going back to Ireland. If that happens, how will I ever see Maureen again? One reason she has not written is that she could not get the penny for the postage. I feel so terrible and here I sit with a shiny dime in my little keepsake box. But I cannot send a dime in the post to Maureen.

That is the bad news of the day: the good news is that Mr. Genovese wants even more of Mama's tortellini.

June 8, 1903

More good news: Luca heard me telling Gabriella about Maureen and how she could not afford to send me letters. So Luca, who knows everything and everybody in the North End, I think, told me about a man whose shoes he shines who keeps carrier pigeons. He said that is the cheap way to send letters — by pigeon.

Bad news: Tomi found out about Mama selling her pasta in the store and she wants Mr. Genovese to keep ten cents and give Mama just ten cents and not seventeen. But Mr. Genovese said no.

June 9, 1903

Luca took me to meet the pigeon man. His name is Gennaro Romagnoli. He lives at the corner of Clark Street very near the waterfront. We went up to the roof of his building and he had at least fifteen coops. And there must have been thirty pigeons, although some were out flying. He asked me where my friend lived — and this is wonderful! He knows a pigeon man in Brooklyn on Maureen's street, Washington Avenue, and from the address it cannot be more than a few blocks from Maureen. For one cent a person can send eight different messages. In other words, one cent buys a person eight pigeon trips. But the problem is that you cannot write much. He showed me the tiny piece of paper that is not much bigger than a stamp. So one must write in the most teeny tiny letters and then it is rolled up and put into a little packet that is attached to the pigeon's leg. However, the pigeon can get to New York within one single day. That is amazing. So I gave him my dime and he gave me back nine pennies, and I sat down and started to write. But it took me a while because I had to think very carefully what to say to Maureen and how to explain all this. So I wrote, *Maureen — this is cheap. Send mail this way. Hope your ma is better. Sofia.* No "Dear" Maureen, no "Love" Sofia.

I can still write long letters to her the expensive way but this might help Maureen. So when I get home I shall send her the translated pages from my diary and then explain more about the pigeon man. Mr. Romagnoli rolled my letter up so tight and he slipped it into a little tube. Next he went to one of his cages and got out a handsome, almost white pigeon that he called Caesar and he strapped the tube to Caesar's leg. We then walked to the edge of the roof. It was beautiful because from there we could see the harbor and the sun was shining. The water was bright blue and there were whitecaps. A two-masted schooner was sailing in smartly with all her canvas flying. Mr. Romagnoli asked me if I wanted to hold Caesar and release him. I was frightened but as soon as Luca said, "I'll do it," I said no, I would. So he showed me how to hold the bird. He was so light but I could feel his little heart that is probably no bigger than a peanut beating fiercely.

Mr. Romagnoli said, "We shall all count to three. When we say three lift up your arms and open your hands. Caesar will take over from there." So we did and I cannot tell you how thrilling this was. One minute I was holding the bird and the next he flew from my hands. For a sliver of a second I felt something fly out of me as if it came from my very soul and joined that of the bird. His tiny heart and mine beating wildly together. I remember what Maureen had said when we last saw one another about distance in miles counting for nothing when indeed we had shared hearts. And now another little heart beats for us in the breast of a pigeon called Caesar.

June 10, 1903

Today I was walking down Hanover Street to meet Chiarina, for she had to take some of her mother's bread to be baked at the shop, and I saw Dr. Balboni. He was standing very still and looked ever so sad. So I stopped and said, "Dr. Balboni, you look so sad."

"Ah, Sofia." He seemed to brighten.

"What is wrong?" I asked.

He then nodded toward the church on the corner of Prince and Hanover. A white hearse, drawn by plumed and harnessed white horses, had just pulled up. I knew the meaning of it.

"A child has died," I whispered.

Dr. Balboni nodded and pressed his lips together until they made a thin gray line. "I suppose it is my lot to witness this since my office is right in the shadow of this great church but this is the second one today. Too many children die."

"But doesn't your milk and baby clinic help?" I asked. "Mama says she has learned so much. She boils all our milk now and scrubs everything with that special soap."

"Yes. But not everyone comes to the clinic, and there are other illnesses that breed in crowded areas and we just do not have the medicines yet for those. Very sad, very sad."

I don't know why, but I suddenly asked if this was the church Dr. Balboni went to, because I never see him at Sacred Heart. And he said something that truly surprised me: "No, I don't go to church."

I don't think I have ever met anyone who does not go to church.

He offered to buy me an ice cream at the Caffe del Sport but I told him I had to meet Chiarina. Then he asked me how my Mama's pasta business was coming. I couldn't help it but I told him Tomi wanted her husband to take more money. He scowled and muttered something under his breath. Maybe I shouldn't have said anything but I know that it is worrying both Papa and Mama. Mr. Genovese tries to be so nice, but Tomi is so awful.

June 11, 1903

Oh, my goodness, it's working. Luca came whooping up the stairs today. In his hand he had a message — a carrier pigeon message — and to think it has only been two days since Caesar flew. This is what the message says: *Ma still very poor. Da had job one day. I quit school to work. Hope.*

I was not sure what she meant by the last word "Hope." Did she mean that there was some hope? That she was hoping? Or, knowing

Maureen, she might be telling me to hope. I think that was it most likely. I am to hope. Hope is sort of like a prayer for Maureen. She believes that you need to hope and pray at the same time. You cannot leave it all to God. She said that was how we got out of quarantine on Ellis Island. So I shall start hoping.

I read the message out loud and Mama and Papa had just been talking about what to do about the pasta for Mr. Genovese. Should they take less money or should Mama try to sell it in another grocery? But when Mama heard this message she said, "For the love of Saint Jude" — Saint Jude is the saint for lost causes — "What are we talking about here? Seven cents less? We are millionaires compared to this poor child's family. I don't want to talk about it anymore, not for now at least. It makes me too sad to think about this poor little family in

Brooklyn and Sofia's very best friend. How would our Sofia ever have lasted in that awful place without Maureen?"

This makes me love Mama so much that I run up to her and throw my arms around her and bury my head against her breast. She smells so good, always of soap and flour. I like this smell better than any perfume.

Later

When Mama said Saint Jude, I remembered something. When I saw Dr. Balboni he was wearing, as he always does, that medal on a chain. It is a long chain and so it is usually tucked into his vest. But today it had come out and I noticed that it was not Saint Christopher on the medal but a star like the six-pointed one that the Jewish girls had on the banner for their club. And then I saw the star on a synagogue on Salem Street, too. I can't figure this out. Is it a new medal? It can't be.

June 12, 1903

The last day of school and guess what Miss Burnet gave me? A book! A book with the whole poem of "The Midnight Ride of Paul Revere." So now I can just go ahead and read the rest of the poem. Miss Burnet says that I should try over the summer vacation to memorize it. There is a school assembly in the autumn that celebrates the day Columbus discovered America and a student is picked to recite this poem that celebrates America's freedom. And best of all, Miss Burnet has sent a note home with me to ask Mama and Papa if she can take me on a visit to Cambridge next week.

June 20, 1903

It is sooooo hot. Went to the meeting of the Lilies of the Arno but it was almost too hot to embroider the flags. We did have big pitchers of lemonade to drink.

Chiarina and I went and bought raspberry ices from the man on the corner of Parmenter and Salem Streets with some of the money we have saved from our lighting the fires at the Cohens' house on their Sabbath.

June 21, 1903

Mama took Gabriella and Luca and Marco and me to the North End Park. There is a beach there where the harbor meets the Charles River. We do not have swimming costumes, but Mama made Gabriella and me wear our petticoats with bloomers and our shirts. There is a barge that people can swim to. It seems to me that all American children know how to swim. We never learned in Cento. But imagine our surprise when we get in the water and suddenly Luca just starts swimming. He swims all the way to the barge. Mama is screaming her head off. And all he does is turn around while he is swimming and say, "Don't worry, Mama. I am good at this!"

I think that Luca has a whole secret life that we know nothing about. Where did he learn to swim?

Later

I forgot to write about Gabriella's idea. She has really learned how to sew very well. She came to me with a grand plan or, as Papa would say, *una grande nozione*. She says that through her sewing teacher she could buy some really nice fabric for a lovely dress for Mama. All she needs is two dollars. And I said that I don't have two dollars. I just have thirty cents from what I have saved from my job. She says if I could give twenty cents she could get the rest from Luca, who makes at least two dollars a week from his jobs. She says that the teacher would help her so she could complete the dress by the mass of the Baptism of the Flags. That is just a week away. I ask how could she ever finish it by then? She blushes and says she has already started. She was just sure that she could get the money and that her teacher loaned her some already and so did Molly. Well, I thought if people Mama does not even know can do this I can, too. It is a wonderful idea. Mama has worn the same two skirts and same two blouses since we got here. Gabriella says the fabric is a deep rose color and will go well with Mama's complexion and be perfect for summer. She secretly measured Mama's blouses and her petticoats and she says it is a loose dress with a belt so it should fit all right. I asked if I could come and watch while she is making it.

June 22, 1903

The dress is absolutely lovely and the teacher, Miss Walker, is so kind. She has a piece of lace that she is giving at no charge to Gabriella to fashion into a collar. Mama is going to look beautiful.

June 26, 1903

The dress is finished. I even helped sew on the buttons. We are trying to figure out how exactly to give it to Mama.

Later

We are going to do it tonight.

Still later

Mama and Papa are arguing. It's about the tortellini. Papa wants Mama to stop selling her tortellini through the Genoveses. He says that Mrs. Genovese is making Mr. Genovese's life miserable and Mama should just take it to Langone's down on Prince Street. Mama says if she does that Mr. Genovese might get mad at Papa because a lot of people are coming into the store to buy it and she doesn't want Papa to get in trouble. Papa says, "We are already in trouble." Finally Gabriella stands up and says, "Please, can I change the subject?" Mama and Papa are startled because children are not supposed to do this. But Gabriella quickly says,

"We have a surprise for you, Mama." Now Mama really looks startled. Gabriella goes and gets the dress. It is wrapped up in tissue paper just like they do at the finest stores. "What is this?" Mama asks as she unwraps the tissue paper. Everyone is so quiet. There are only the whisking sounds of tissue paper and our breathing.

"*Che cosa straordinaria!*" Mama exclaims.

"A dress for you, Mama," Gabriella says. "I made it."

"I paid for it," Luca breaks in.

"Me, too!" I say, thinking of my twenty cents.

Mama begins to cry. Even Papa is leaking tears. Marco starts to eat the tissue paper. There is no more talk of the price of tortellini.

June 30, 1903

Mama was so beautiful in church for the Baptism of the Flags, and you should have seen the look on Tomi's face!

July 1, 1903

Tomorrow I go to Cambridge with Miss Burnet. I am so excited. I am to meet her in North Square by the bank and then we are going to walk to Haymarket, the big market, and take a hack from there to Cambridge. In all the months I have been here I have never been out of the North End, and now I am to cross the Charles River to Cambridge. I think even Luca has not traveled this far.

July 3, 1903

Cambridge is so lovely. There are big houses and big trees. We walked up Brattle Street and saw where Henry Longfellow the poet had lived, and then we walked through Harvard Yard. But most exciting, Miss Burnet took me to her father's office in the Harvard observatory. Dr. Burnet is very very tall. He reminds me of a bird — not a pigeon, but one of those birds with long stalky legs. And his nose is like a beak. He wears tiny spectacles and looked over them at me as if he were peering at something very small but interesting.

He showed me the telescope and explained the mirrors and how they work and then he showed me star charts. He has devoted most of his life to the study of something called nebulas, which are gases and dust that surround stars. I could have talked to him forever, and luckily he walked back with us from the observatory to their house on Scott Street. In his study he showed me more star charts and even some photographs that were taken through a telescope of things called star clusters and our own galaxy — the Milky Way. I had never even known that our Earth was part of something called a galaxy named the Milky Way.

For lunch they served chicken salad and iced tea and Mrs. Burnet was so nice to me but all I wanted to do was hear Dr. Burnet talk about the sky. He promised me that I could come back some night, "when the heavens are active," as he put it, and together we can look through the big telescope and study what he called "the souls of the night."

Later

I am making a list of all my new astronomy words: galaxy, nebula, meteor, magnitude (that is the brightness of a star).

I think, though, that the most exciting thing that I learned from Dr. Burnet was that Earth is a very teeny tiny little planet in what he calls "a very insignificant galaxy." We really are not the center of anything. He thinks it is absolutely silly that Boston calls itself "the Hub" as it does, as if all the world revolves around us. He snorted just the way Mama snorts.

July 5, 1903

I rode on the float with the other Lilies of the Arno in the Fourth of July parade. We all waved our flags. It was fun but I just cannot stop thinking about my trip to Cambridge. I also keep remembering what Dr. Balboni asked me — what did I want to be? Well, maybe I want to be an astronomer and study the souls of the night. Now that is something that is more than just a job.

July 6, 1903

Starting to worry again about Maureen. I have written her and sent off Caesar twice in the last week and a half but still no answer. What if she went back to Ireland and did not have time to send a message?

July 7, 1903

Very hot again. Fredo, the little boy who lives down the hall, said his father plays the mandolin, so tonight we all went up on the roof of our building and listened while he played. Mama and Papa sang some old songs from Cento. It was a very starry night and I wondered if Dr. Burnet was looking through his telescope. I have taken a book from the lending library at the Bennet Street School that tells all about the stars, and I am trying to figure out the constellations. I found the Big Dipper and the Little Dipper, and if you follow straight out from the last star in the cup of the Big Dipper you can find the North Star, which I did. But now I am looking for some of the other constellations like Cassiopeia and Orion's Belt.

July 9, 1903

Terrible heat. Went swimming but it didn't make me that much cooler. Came back with a headache.

Later

I feel absolutely awful. Mama just went to get Dr. Balboni. Can't write.

August 9, 1903

This is the first day in a month I have written. I am in a bed at the Massachusetts General Hospital. I have caught a terrible disease. Dr. Balboni calls it infantile paralysis. I nearly died. My left leg is weak. A nurse must help me walk. Mama sits and cries.

August 10, 1903

Mama's tortellini business is over. She could not cook and take care of me and the rest of the family. I am scared to ask if the pigeon has come with a message from Maureen.

All the news seems so bad. A lady is coming today to fit my leg with a brace. My leg is ugly. Very, very skinny. Dr. Balboni tries to cheer me up. None of his jokes work.

August 11, 1903

Dr. Balboni says tomorrow I can go home. I guess I should be happy but I limp now. I must use a crutch. Sometimes I fall down. He says I shall be better.

Later

Miss Burnet came to visit me. She says that I can still come to Cambridge. She gave me a letter from her father. It makes me feel better than any medicine. Here is what it says:

Dear Sofia,

I was shocked and saddened to hear of your illness. When you are well, which I trust shall be soon, we would like you to come to Cambridge again. This time you may spend the night and we shall go to the observatory. The Perseid showers shall begin in about ten days — these are the nights of the shooting stars. But we can also explore the dark spaces between the stars and hunt for new galaxies. We can look for those dusty cobwebs that signal nebula and then deep within it find a bright, bright star caught like a beautiful insect in a spider's net. Get well and come to Cambridge.

Fondly,
William Burnet

August 20, 1903

I have been home a week now. Everyone says my walking has improved. I hate to use the crutch but I need to. It is very hard for me to get up the stairs to our apartment, so I have only been out twice. Dr. Balboni comes every day. He is going to send a nurse to show Mama how to massage my leg and how to do some exercises to make it stronger.

Mama is cooking again some. And Papa is taking her tortellini to the grocery. There are no problems now as Mrs. Genovese is still "up north." Still no word from Maureen. I wrote her a letter and told her about my infantile paralysis. You would think that would get her to write. I am sure she has left to go home to Ireland.

Chiarina came to visit and she brought a basket of candy and cookies from the Lilies of the Arno. I missed the Saint Anthony's feast day. It seems now that there are feast days every Saturday. You can hear the bells in the Old North Church ringing as the statues of the saints pass, and you can hear all the noise from the streets. I don't want to go down, though. I don't like being out in crowds with my crutch. I like it, though, when everyone else goes and I am alone. I can practice my walking in peace. No one to watch. Mama winces every time she sees me almost lose balance.

August 21, 1903

Tomorrow I am supposed to go to Cambridge. Dr. Balboni has offered to take me there. I have funny feelings. I want to go and yet I don't. Miss Burnet really wants me to come. She says she has fixed up the guest room for me.

I really don't want to go.

August 22, 1903

Dr. Balboni came to pick me up and Mama told him I didn't want to go. His face turned very stern. I have never seen Dr. Balboni look so fierce. He asked to speak to me alone. So Mama took Marco out and Gabriella excused herself. Then he spoke to me very sharply. "Sofia, you are a smart girl. You have a brain. You speak beautiful English, and do you know what you are becoming?"

"What?" I asked.

"One withered leg!" There was something so shocking about these three words. "Are you not more than that? Is this not an insult to the God that made you?"

I could not help it, but the words just slipped out. "But Dr. Balboni, you don't even believe in God."

"What are you talking about?"

"You said yourself you don't go to church."

"I can believe in God without going to church. I believe in all gods. That is why I wear this medal." And he dug into his vest and pulled out the medallion. "You see Saint Christopher on one side. The Star of David on the other. I believe in it all. When I eat your mother's tortellini I say a little prayer — a little tortellini prayer. I see God in that tortellini. I say, "My God, there is a God, for you created this woman who makes the best tortellini on earth. My tongue is blessed with each bite."

I had never heard such talk in my life. I nodded and said, "All right, Dr. Balboni. I shall go to Cambridge."

How can I argue with a man like this?

August 25, 1903

Tonight I have come back from Cambridge. I saw through the telescope the streamers of the Milky Way that wave softly in the darkness. I saw distant stars like murmurs in the night. Their light was faint but Dr. Burnet told me that this light coming to Earth started hundreds of thousands of years ago. And here I was to see it, to catch it first in the telescope! I wondered if Christopher Columbus felt this way when he first saw America. He saw the land rising from the sea and he must have gasped the way I did when I saw this light that had traveled so far. And right now I went to the roof — yes, sort of climbed, sort of crawled. Luca and I are sitting here and the moon is just an eyelash, but to me the whole sky begins to whisper its secrets. And yes, I am much more than just a withered leg. Dr. Balboni was right.

August 27, 1903

When I came back from the meeting of the Lilies of the Arno, Dr. Balboni was sitting at the table with Mama and Papa. They were having a serious discussion. I was so worried at first, I thought it was something about me — my leg. Maybe I would have to have an operation or something. Or maybe I had not been doing my exercises right. But it was not about me. It was about Mama. Dr. Balboni wants Mama to open a pasta shop. I never knew this but he owns several buildings in the North End and he has bought a new one on Prince Street near his office. There is space on the ground floor for a shop. Dr. Balboni will rent it to Mama and Papa very reasonably and he will also lend them money to start the business. But this is not just to be a tortellini and pasta business. Dr. Balboni wants Papa to start importing some tomatoes, canned tomatoes from Cento. And he thinks other things as well. It would be like a *salumeria*, a delicatessen. Papa and Mama say they must think about it.

Later

Gabriella and Luca and I think Mama and Papa should accept Dr. Balboni's offer. We tell Mama and Papa. And they say it is a big risk. We are a poor family. We cannot take such risks. I think they have to. I am so frightened that they won't.

August 29, 1903

I have done something probably very bad. Mama and Papa would just die if they found out I did such a thing. But I had to. I think the thing that made me do it was that I saw Tomi in the street. She pretended not to see me but I know she did. I could not bear to think of Papa working in their grocery any longer. So I went directly to Dr. Balboni's office.

"What is it?" he asked when he saw me.

"Give Mama and Papa the withered leg talk."

Now it was Dr. Balboni's turn to be surprised.

"What are you talking about, Sofia?"

"You know the talk," I said. "They can't decide whether to do what you want them to do. They keep talking about the risks and every day there seems to be a new reason why they shouldn't do it."

"But what does a withered leg have to do with it? They might have very good reasons not to do this."

"No, they don't. They are using the reasons the way I used my withered leg. It's an excuse."

Dr. Balboni pulled down his mouth as if he were considering what I said. "You are a very forward child. You know that, Sofia?"

"Yes, I know it. Good-bye." And I sort of waved at him with my crutch as I limped out the door.

September 4, 1903

School starts in four days. Still no word from Maureen. But some very good news. Mama and Papa have decided to take Dr.

Balboni's offer. Now if I could only hear that Maureen is all right and know that Mama and Papa's shop will work I wouldn't even mind limping for the rest of my life, which I probably will anyhow.

September 5, 1903

Papa told Mr. Genovese that he is leaving. Mr. Genovese seemed sad but was understanding. He said that he did not think he would tell his wife Mama and Papa's plans for a while. Papa thinks that is a good idea.

September 8, 1903

Best news: Miss Burnet is to be the fifth grade teacher this year. My teacher. Oh, I am so happy. And guess what? I am to recite "The

Midnight Ride of Paul Revere" at the Columbus Day assembly.

September 17, 1903

A letter from Maureen. She must have spent their last penny to send it. Maureen's mother has died. She and her father and her brothers and sisters leave for Ireland in two weeks. I start crying and cannot stop. Mama is so upset. She knows how much I love Maureen.

September 20, 1903

I have the best Mama. She says that she is going to write to Maureen's father and see if perhaps he would consider allowing Maureen to come to Boston and live with us. Mama thinks that we could fit another very narrow bed into the room where Gabriella and I sleep.

I can't believe Mama would do this. I am helping her with the letter.

We are also going to send a message by carrier pigeon, which will get there faster. We must catch them before they go back.

Mama says she is going to talk to Dr. Balboni about it to see if he might have some ideas, to.

At least I can hope now. And I shall hope the way Maureen has taught me to hope. Like an athlete. That is how Maureen hopes. Her hoping has muscles.

September 23, 1903

We haven't heard anything from Maureen or her father. Mama keeps telling me not to get my hopes up. But I really don't know how one can stop hoping.

I told Miss Burnet about Maureen. She says

she will keep her fingers crossed. So that's hoping.

I am practicing reciting "The Midnight Ride of Paul Revere." But it's hard to think about it when I am so busy hoping.

September 27, 1903

Mama and Papa have the shop all ready to open. Luca has gone around the North End and put up signs. Gabriella and I worked all day Saturday helping them scrub and clean and paint. It looks all sparkling and shiny. Mama's first batch of pasta is ready. She made three kinds for the opening — tagliatelle, tortellini, and gnocchi. But she is going to make others, too.

October 2, 1903

I am still hoping for Maureen but I can tell that Mama doesn't believe she will come. She says things like, "It is hard for a father to give up his daughter." I say, "But he has fifteen children — what's just one?" Mama looks at me and almost snorts. I know I should not bother her with this talk now, as she is so busy with the shop.

October 10, 1903

I couldn't write for a few days because we spent a lot of time in school practicing for the assembly. My reciting the poem is just one small part of the whole assembly. There is a play and Chiarina's older brother Pauli is Christopher Columbus. I have helped to paint the scenery. We have made from cardboard the hull of a ship, and then we used broomsticks and attached sails to them. It looks good. I am getting pretty excited about this. I have never been in a performance before. Unless you call my First Communion a performance. No scenery, though, and I didn't have to stand up and recite a whole long poem.

October 14, 1903

I cannot believe what I am about to write. In my own bed next to me Maureen sleeps. Dr. Balboni says he will get another bed for us tomorrow, but as far as I care she can sleep next to me always. I cannot believe this. Some might say it is a miracle but maybe it is just hard hoping that did it. Here is what happened. Mama had said that she could not leave the shop to come to the school assembly for the Columbus Day program. I had just gotten to the last verse of the poem. I was saying,

So through the night rode Paul Revere;
And so through the night went his cry
of alarm
To every Middlesex village and farm.

I saw some people enter at the back of the hall, but I was up on the stage and really couldn't see. I continued reciting, "In the hour of darkness and peril . . . ," but I felt something. There was something in the room. A feeling in my heart. It was so odd. I thought of the feeling I had when I held the pigeon Caesar in my hands. The beating of his fast little heart. The thrill of his flight as he left my hands. I knew then that Maureen was here!

And when the lights came up, there she was standing between Mama and Dr. Balboni, and next to Dr. Balboni was our old friend Father Finnegan. And Maureen was the same Maureen, her skin so pale and her hair so red. She stood like a small lick of fire. And once more, like the first time I ever saw her on Ellis Island, I was drawn to that flame like a moth on a summer's night. I didn't even need my crutch. I felt my feet walking straight to her, and I thought what a perfect day for Maureen to come here — Columbus Day. Together we shall rediscover America, but it will be all new for us!

Historical Note

The North End, the oldest neighborhood in Boston, is the city's historic heart. It was there that the American Revolution was first organized by Paul Revere, Samuel Adams, and John Hancock.

Quincy Market

First settled by the Puritans in the early 1600s, all kinds of businesses sprang up there. The North End continued to expand throughout the eighteenth and nineteenth centuries, as merchants, shopkeepers, and tradesmen came there to do business.

As Boston's port grew larger, immigrants began to pour into the city. By the middle of the nineteenth century, the North End was the most densely populated neighborhood in the city. Between 1900 and 1920, the immigrant population of the North End grew from 28,000 to 40,000 — and many of them were Italians.

Tenements were built at an increasing speed so that the influx of immigrants could find housing. The extremely rapid increase in population left the city unprepared, and the streets of the North End grew crowded and dirty, and disease became widespread.

Dr. Gerardo Balboni, the grandfather of author Kathryn Lasky's husband, was a well-known figure amoung the immigrant communities of Boston, expecially in the North End. Dr. Balboni was an Italian immigrant who made his mission to train immigrant parents

Dr. Gerardo Balboni with his patients

in hygiene and general health care. In the early 1900s, he opened a well baby clinic in the North End to teach mothers how to protect their children from serious diseases, contaminated foods, and unclean tenements.

Immigrants, who often came from rural communities, also needed help learning to adjust to life in a big city. The North Bennet Street Industrial School was founded in 1885 for children and women who could go there to study English, sewing, cleaning, and other skills that would allow them to find jobs to help support their families.

Women and girls study sewing

Boston's North End immigrant population became a very important part of the city's life and history. But it was the Italian immigrants who would shape this neighborhood. As they made their homes there, cafés, delicatessens, and Italian groceries would start filling the sidewalks, and as they struggled to learn English, and to go to work and school — to be American — they would give the North End a distinctly Italian feel, which remains today.

About the Author

Kathryn Lasky is the author of more than forty books for children and adults, including the first book of Sofia's Immigrant Diary, *Hope in My Heart*. She has also written four books for the Dear America series: *A Journey to the New World*, *Dreams in the Golden Country*, *Christmas After All*, and *A Time for Courage*. She is also the author of Newbery Honor book *Sugaring Time*.

Acknowledgments

Grateful acknowledgment is made for permission to reprint the following:

Cover Portrait by Glenn Harrington
Page 103: Quincy Market, North Wind Picture Archives, Alfred, Maine.
Page 105: Dr. Gerardo Balboni with patients, Courtesy of Kathryn Lasky.
Page 106: Women and girls study sewing, Lewis Hine/CORBIS, New York.

Other books in the My America series

Corey's Underground Railroad Diaries
by Sharon Dennis Wyeth

Elizabeth's Jamestown Colony Diaries
by Patricia Hermes

Hope's Revolutionary War Diaries
by Kristiana Gregory

Joshua's Oregon Trail Diaries
by Patricia Hermes

Meg's Prairie Diaries
by Kate McMullan

Sofia's Immigrant Diaries
by Kathryn Lasky

Virginia's Civil War Diaries
by Mary Pope Osborne

Library of Congress Cataloging-in-Publication Data
Lasky, Kathryn.
Home at last / by Kathryn Lasky.
p.   cm. — (My America) (Sofia's immigrant diary ; bk. 2)
Summary: In 1903, ten-year-old Sofia and her family begin their life in America in Boston,
where her father works in a grocery, her mother sells pasta, and she goes to school while
trying to stay in touch with her old friend Maureen. Includes historical notes.
ISBN 0-439-44963-4; 0-439-20644-8 (pbk.)
[1. Immigrants — Fiction.   2. Italian Americans — Fiction.   3. Diaries — Fiction.
4. Boston (Mass.) — History — 1865 — Fiction.]
I. Title.   II. Series
PZ7.L3274 Hm 2003
[Fic] 21   2002044514
CIP   AC

10 9 8 7 6 5 4 3 2   04 05 06 07

The display type was set in Edwardian Medium.
The text type was set in Goudy.
Photo research by Amla Sanghvi.
Book design by Elizabeth B. Parisi.

Printed in the U.S.A.   23
First edition, November 2003

FIC LAS - Home at Last

DATE DUE
